YOU HAVE ARRIVED
AT YOUR DESTINATION

Copyright © 2020 by Independent Bookstore Day Publishing

First (and only) Edition

Printed in the United States of America for Independent Bookstore Day

Cover and interior design: Kristine N. Brogno

ISBN 978-1-7329704-0-3

Originally published as part of the Forward collection by Amazon Original Stories.
This work remains the property of the author.

Independent Bookstore Day would like to thank Mr. Towles and his agent
Dorain Karchmar for the use of this work and for their dedicated and continued
support of independent bookstores.

Independent Bookstore Day Publishing
A program of the American Booksellers Association
www.indiebookstoreday.com

YOU HAVE ARRIVED AT YOUR DESTINATION

AMOR TOWLES

INDEPENDENT
BOOKSTORE DAY
SATURDAY, APRIL 25, 2020

YOU HAVE ARRIVED AT YOUR DESTINATION

IT HAD BEEN YEARS since Sam had been this far out on the expressway. For a few summers when he was a boy—before his family moved out west—they had driven almost to the end of it on their way to a seaside rental on Orient Point. At the time, there was nothing from Exit 40 to Exit 60, not even a gas station. Each of the off-ramps led to a little tree-lined road that led to a little tree-lined town with its own movie theater, pharmacy, and hardware store. When Sam was twenty-two, he traveled it again to spend Labor Day weekend with a college roommate. By then, every few exits you would come upon a cluster of big-box stores like AutoZone, Home Depot, and Toys "R" Us—the category killers designed to make the small towns even smaller. Now, twenty-three years later, Sam was paying witness to the latest phase in the expressway's evolution: the so-called Millennium Miles. Thanks to a demographic analysis that sought to maximize proximity to an educated workforce, a university center, and reasonably priced housing, various members of the "new economy" had opened large, gleaming facilities along this stretch of road.

In one mile, take Exit 46, then bear left, said the pleasant voice of the GPS.

Earlier that month, having told Annie that he didn't want anything for his birthday, Sam had bought himself a Model S. The car had cost him more than he'd intended to spend, but as his colleague covering luxury goods never tired of observing: You get what you pay for. The Model S could accelerate from zero to sixty in two seconds, travel three hundred miles without a recharge, and the engine had been designed with such care, you could hardly hear it hum. It also came with a self-driving system. By means of cameras mounted on the four corners of the car, it could follow roadways, moderate speed, make turns. The sales consultant at the dealership had conceded that it wasn't quite foolproof yet (there had been a fatality, in fact). So, the official recommendation was to use the system with one's hands on the wheel, one's foot on the brake, and one's eye on the road. For the fun of it, Sam took his hands off the wheel and his foot off the gas, then watched as the blinker turned on, the engine decelerated, and the car followed its own instructions onto the off-ramp. Bearing left, the car passed over the expressway, took another left onto an access road, and a right into a parking lot.

You have arrived at your destination.

Sam wasn't particularly surprised to find that Vitek had a crowded parking lot. But as he reassumed control of the car and steered toward the building's entrance, he was surprised to find just six spaces reserved for customers, three of which were empty. Sam knew that Vitek's services were expensive; he just didn't know how expensive. When Annie had returned from an introductory meeting saying that the price was almost "unconscionable," he had brushed the matter of expense aside. But having done so, he felt that to wade back into specifics would have diminished the nobility of his gesture. So he had never found out the actual price. That only three customers were currently shouldering the entire cost structure in front of him probably didn't bode well. But then, by all accounts, at Vitek you got what you paid for too.

The clock on the dashboard indicated that Sam was a few minutes early. Looking through the windshield he saw a sunlit sitting area just outside the main entrance, where some younger employees (or associates or stakeholders) were drinking coffee by a fountain.

Sam shook his head.

In the last decade, he had visited hundreds of regional power companies across the country. The meetings with management generally took place in offices that could have been in the administration suite of a public high school from the 1960s—with gray, synthetic carpets, ceiling tiles, and fluorescent lights. Sam always took some comfort from the outmoded décor because there was no better predictor of an earnings disappointment than a brand-new corporate headquarters. And while one "disruptive" business model would inevitably replace another, the good old power company would always be there to turn on the lights.

From the passenger seat came the ting of a text message. Picking up his phone, Sam saw that it was from Annie: *Have Fun!*

Sam typed: *Will do*

Then after a moment, he added a reciprocal exclamation point.

ORIENTATION

AT THE FRONT DESK, Sam gave his name to an attractive young woman wearing a wireless headset. She promised that someone would be with him in a moment and invited him to take a seat. Sam chose one of the Mies van der Rohe chairs arranged around the white marble coffee table. From somewhere in the sunlit lobby came the sound of moving water.

"Is there a waterfall in here?" he asked.

The woman at the front desk looked up. "Excuse me?"

He gestured around the lobby with a smile. "I can hear the sound of water."

Smiling back, she pointed outside. "Dr. Gerhardt had a microphone put in the fountain so that the sound could be piped in. Isn't it soothing?"

Before Sam could answer, another attractive young woman— this one in a black skirt suit, holding a black portfolio—emerged from an elevator.

"Mr. Paxton?" she asked.

"Yes."

"I'm Sybilla. I work with Mr. Owens. Won't you come this way?"

Sybilla took Sam up to the third floor. When the elevator door opened, there was the distinct smell of popcorn. Sam wondered if Dr. Gerhardt was having that piped in too. But as they passed through a sitting area, he saw the brightly lit carnival-style popcorn machine in the corner.

"I think you're really going to enjoy meeting Mr. Owens," Sybilla said with what appeared to be genuine enthusiasm. "He's been with Vitek practically since the beginning. No one knows the company better."

She led Sam through an open-plan workspace to a small conference room with a flat-screen television mounted on the wall. At her invitation, Sam took a seat. It was one of those ergonomic office chairs that rock and spin.

"Would you like some coffee? Sparkling water?"

"I'm fine, thanks."

"Mr. Owens will be joining you in just a few minutes. I'm sure you've read our brochure and that your wife has told you all about our work, but while you wait, Mr. Owens thought you might want to watch a short introductory film on the company."

Without waiting for a reply, Sybilla opened her portfolio, which turned out to be an iPad, and tapped on the screen. The television on the wall lit up with the company's logo and, as she quietly closed the door behind her, the video began.

"Welcome to Vitek," said a voice that was at once friendly, assured, and upbeat. What followed was a typical ten-minute informational video, complete with photographic shots of Dr. Gerhardt and his partners as younger men, an animated graphic of a spinning double helix, clips of white-coated technicians in labs, news of a breakthrough, and testimonials from "actual" customers as indicated by the names, ages, and cities of residence at the bottom of the screen.

Sam hadn't actually gotten around to reading the brochure, but the video recapped what he had gathered from Annie. A twenty-first-century fertility lab, Vitek had combined the decoding of the human genome and recent advances in behavioral science to help couples not simply become pregnant but to give them some influence over the intelligence and temperament of their child. When the company's logo returned to the screen, the conference room's door was simultaneously knocked upon and opened. In walked a good-looking man who was a little bit taller than Sam, and maybe a little bit younger too.

"Sam!" he said with a hand outstretched. "HT Owens. It's so good to meet you."

Sam stood and shook HT's hand, thinking his voice sounded familiar. It took him a moment to realize that it sounded familiar because it was the voice of the narrator in the video he'd just watched.

HT sat down and immediately rocked back and forth in his chair, making the most of its engineering. Then he drummed the top of the table with his open hands. Sam suspected that if HT had been born a generation later than he was, he would have been raised on Ritalin.

"Did you have any trouble finding us?"

"Not at all."

"Great."

He pointed at the logo on the screen. "And you got a chance to watch the video?"

"I did."

"Great. Let me start by saying how much fun we've had getting to know Annie. You're a lucky man!"

"Thanks," replied Sam, though it had always seemed to him that the observation of a man's luck in regard to his wife was a bit of a slight.

HT shifted gears. "I don't have to explain to you why you're here, Sam. You *know* why you're here. And you've been a utilities analyst for, what? Almost twenty years? So, I think we can skip the dog and pony show. Instead, let me give you a quick overview of our work, then we can talk about what's going to happen today. Sound good?"

"Sounds good."

"Great," said HT for the third time. "Now, we all understand that child development is a combination of nature and nurture, and for hundreds of years, parents have sought to influence both of these factors for the benefit of their offspring. From the genetic standpoint, we have carefully selected our mate with his or her attributes firmly in mind. While from the nurture standpoint, once we've had children, we have tried to provide them with a healthy environment, a strong education, and a system of values. Why do we do this? So that our offspring can lead happy and productive lives. Well, Vitek was launched in recognition of the fact that, given recent advances in various fields of science, parents can now pursue this goal with an unprecedented level of intentionality."

"Through genetic engineering," Sam said.

HT put up both hands in soft protest. "We don't really think of our work here as genetic engineering, Sam. We're not brewing things up in a lab. We're not going to introduce any new elements into your DNA, nor are we going to take any existing elements out. Rather, having taken a peek into the traits that your child will naturally receive, with your and Annie's guidance we're going to push a few into the forefront and a few into the background. We like to think of it as *genetic nudging.*"

"Okay," said Sam.

"But that's only *half* the picture. You see, what we've done here—what's so unusual about our approach—is that we've combined the genetic component with predictive modeling founded on large pools of demographic data."

HT paused.

"Do you know what a credit score is?"

Sam was a little surprised by the question.

"It's a tool the banks use," he said after a moment, "to determine creditworthiness."

"Exactly," said HT. "But do you know how it works?"

Sam had to admit he didn't, so HT obliged.

"The credit score was invented in the late 1980s by a mathematician and an engineer who realized that by analyzing historical patterns of consumer debt repayment they could design algorithms that could predict an individual's reliability as a mortgagee. For simplicity's sake, let's say you examine the credit histories of ten thousand Americans who, twenty years ago, with similar incomes, expenses, and credit card balances all took out fifteen-year mortgages. In looking at this cohort, what you discover is that virtually everyone who borrowed two hundred thousand dollars to buy a house ended up repaying the loan in full, while only half of those who borrowed three hundred thousand dollars to buy a bigger house succeeded in doing so. And those who borrowed four hundred thousand dollars to buy an even bigger house? Nearly every one of them defaulted. Practically speaking, what this means is that if I identify someone today with a similar profile to that cohort (making some adjustments for inflation and what-have-you), without even having to talk to him I know that if I loan him two hundred grand to buy a home, he'll repay me, if I loan him three hundred grand, he might, and if I loan him four hundred grand, he won't. The *pattern* becomes *predictive.*"

HT held out his upturned hands as if to say: *Voilà.*

"We are doing the same thing here, Sam, but instead of looking at aggregated financial histories to anticipate individual financial outcomes, we are looking at aggregated biographic histories to predict individual biographic outcomes. Drawing from a wide array of sources, we've assembled a database on three generations of Americans, which includes not only their gender and ethnicity but information on the environments in which they were raised—like their parents' religions, educations, professions, and political identifications. Then we have traced how the lives of the subjects actually unfolded. By mapping the foundational information of this large population alongside their eventual experiences, we can start to identify meaningful patterns that help us clarify how nature and nurture have combined to shape the lives they've led."

The door opened and Sybilla came in with a small ceramic cup and a thick green file, both of which she set on the table in front of HT.

"Were you offered something to drink? Do you want an espresso?"

"I'm good, thanks."

Sybilla exited.

"Where was I?"

"The lives they've led ..."

"Right! So, let's turn our attention to you and Annie. What we do here, is we take the science I've just described, and we apply it to an individual case like yours. We use our analysis of your and Annie's genomes along with a little nudging to refine the traits your child is going to be born with. We use the detailed profiles you've given us on yourselves to understand the environment in which your child will be raised. Then by using those elements as a filter, we can identify within our proprietary database a significant cohort of people with a similar genetic makeup who were brought up in a similar environment and, based on their actual experiences, begin to anticipate—within a margin of acceptable error—the shape of the life that *your* child will lead."

Having slowly leaned closer and closer to the table as he delivered this speech, HT now sat back in his chair and smiled.

"Crazy, right?"

Sam found himself sitting back in his chair too.

In retrospect, he'd had no idea of what to expect from this meeting. When Annie had first suggested (in a rather emotional conversation) that maybe it was time to try IVF, it was Sam who had suggested they turn to Vitek—having heard about it from a colleague in the life-science area, and then from a wealthy client who was a happy customer. But Sam hadn't talked to either of them about the company in much detail. Once he and Annie had decided to go forward, he had filled out all of Vitek's question-naires to the best of his ability and dutifully generated a specimen at their lab in the city. But, up until this afternoon, he had assumed that he and Annie would be able to pick their child's sex, eliminate the risk of birth defects, and maybe get a marginal boost in IQ. A leg up in a competitive world, as it were. Not unlike sending your kid to a private school, or securing him a well-placed internship. But what HT was talking about seemed like a far more elaborate value proposition …

"Pretty crazy," Sam agreed after a moment.

"Crazy *amazing!*" HT said with a smile. Then he shifted gears again. "I know you've been on the road for the last few weeks. So, while we've gathered all your background materials, we haven't had a chance to talk about options. The good news is that Annie

has done a lot of the legwork for you. She's spent hours here meeting with me and a few of the other counselors going through our
catalog of profiles, and she has narrowed the opportunity set down
to three choices for you to consider."

HT paused for emphasis.

"I've got to give your wife a lot of credit, Sam. Most people
who narrow our universe down to three choices for the benefit
of their husband or their wife make a classic mistake: They end
up with three candidates who, in the grand scheme of things, are
virtually identical. In a way, they've already made the choice about
the child they want to raise, they just haven't gotten around to
telling their spouse."

HT gave Sam a wink.

"But Annie …" HT laid a hand on the file that was still sitting
beside his untouched espresso. "She has chosen three very distinct
profiles. I mean, these three are totally different people who would
lead totally different lives, and yet would all be children whom
you two would be proud to have raised. Now, at this point, I could
hand you our detailed biographs to give you a sense of the three
candidates, but we've found that it's hard for most people to trans-
late all the relevant data into a mental picture. So, what we've done
is we've taken the information in the biographs and translated it
into three short films which will introduce you to the three different

children that, with our assistance, you and Annie could have. We call them *projections*. The films are each just a few minutes long, but they should give you plenty to think about, so that you and Annie can make the best possible choice."

HT slapped the table once. "What do you say, Sam? Are you ready?"

"I'm ready."

"Then let's do it!"

PROJECTION
ONE

GRABBING THE THICK GREEN FILE, HT leapt from his chair and led Sam down the hall, waving to colleagues as he went. Somewhere in the middle of the building, he opened a door and motioned for Sam to enter. Inside, there was a well-appointed screening room with sixteen upholstered viewing chairs in a four-by-four grid.

HT noticed Sam raising his eyebrows at the number of chairs.

"Sometimes our clients bring family or friends to the viewing," he explained. "But between you and me, I'm not sure it's a great idea. I mean, it's hard enough debating with your family and friends what you're going to *name* your kid, right? Never mind getting into nuances of personality and potential."

A young man appeared dressed in the black pants and white shirt of a waiter at a catered affair. HT turned to Sam.

"You sure you don't want something to drink? A cappuccino? Some water? A gin and tonic … ?"

At the words "gin and tonic," Sam must have expressed surprise, because HT smiled a little slyly.

"That's your drink, right?" By way of explanation, he raised the green file, then he shifted to a more serious tone. "I know it's not quite five o'clock, but we find that having a drink can be very additive to the experience. It relaxes you a little, so you can sit back and enjoy the process—which is important. Because you should enjoy this process."

"One gin and tonic," said Sam.

"Make it two, James!"

James returned a moment later with two gin and tonics in crystal highball glasses—not unlike the ones that Annie and Sam had registered for when they were married. Sam wondered if that was in the file too.

For the third time in an hour, Sam was offered a seat and he took it. Just as in the conference room, the screening chairs swung and tilted and, once again, HT made the most of their engineering.

"Cheers!" HT said.

"Cheers."

The two clinked glasses, then HT tilted his head in the direction of the projection booth. "Okay, Harry. Let her rip."

As the lights dimmed, Sam took a swig from his drink and leaned back in his chair, having to admit that it was surprisingly comfortable. As before, the Vitek logo filled the screen, but this time it began shrinking as if it were fading into the distance until it finally disappeared. After a suitable passage of time—just long enough to forget the logo, but not long enough to become antsy—a single word appeared center-screen: *Daniel*.

A little startled, Sam turned to HT, who smiled and nodded. Right from the beginning, Sam and Annie had decided they would have a boy, but there had been some debate over his name. Annie had wanted to name him after her father, Andy, and Sam had wanted to name him after his uncle, Daniel—both of whom had died in recent years. Sam was touched that Annie had settled on Daniel without saying anything.

The opening shot of the projection was a brand-new baby swaddled in a light-blue blanket. Though the person holding the baby was not in the frame, it was clear from his hands that it was a man, presumably the father. The baby was not crying. He wasn't squinting or squirming. Rather, as the female narrator observed: *From the day he was born, Daniel had a smile on his face.*

As the narrator went on to describe young Daniel's good nature and his positive outlook, there were clips of him at the age of eight giving a hand to a friend at the playground, at the age of fifteen setting the table for dinner, and at the age of twenty-two on the quad of an old New England college surrounded by friends, tossing his cap in the air as his parents looked proudly on.

Sam felt something of a jolt when he realized that the parents, whose backs were to the camera, looked like an older version of him and Annie. But of course they did. This was supposed to be *their* child. And the hands in the opening shot hadn't simply been "the father's" hands, they'd been *his* hands. The realization made Sam sit up a little in his chair.

Daniel is now behind the wheel of a beat-up station wagon with a pretty young blonde in the passenger seat and cardboard boxes in back. As they come over a bridge, the two lean forward and look up through the windshield at the skyscrapers of a metropolitan center. They pull up in front of a narrow six-story building, the sort of low-rent walk-up in which young urbanites begin their adult lives. With a box in his arms, Daniel holds the door open with his shoulder to let his girlfriend inside. Next, Daniel is standing before the entrance of a modern office building called the Century Tower. After double-checking the address in his hand, Daniel gazes up at the building's gleaming facade then gamely goes through the revolving door.

Despite knowing perfectly well that this entire production was a contrivance, Sam felt a certain sense of optimism, maybe even pride, when he saw Daniel looking through the windshield with his pretty girlfriend, when he held the door open for her, and when he entered his shiny new office building. These feelings harmonized with the warm buzzing that he had begun to feel in his head from the gin.

Upstairs, Daniel is shown by his boss to his cubicle, where he is introduced to a colleague—another young man in his early twenties, who, you can just tell, is going to be Daniel's first friend in the city. And as Daniel sits down ready to get to work, the narrator confirms that Daniel is beginning his new life *with the same good nature and positive outlook that had characterized him since the day he was born.*

But even as the narrator completed this sentence, there was a shot of cumulus clouds rolling over Century Tower in accelerated motion, and the background music took on a more ominous tone. Then the narrator qualified her previous remark by observing that *not everyone in Daniel's circle was as happy-go-lucky.*

A quick series of scenes reveals that some of Daniel's peers are, in fact, more ambitious, more focused, more cutthroat. The sequence culminates in a shot of Daniel's "first friend" stopping by Daniel's desk to drop off a stack of files for processing. The camera closes in on a clock on the wall, the hands of which start spinning faster and faster until they blur and then come to a stop at six o'clock. The camera pulls back to reveal Daniel at the same desk but in his early thirties. Another pile of work to be processed is dropped off by a different colleague, who is noticeably younger than Daniel.

It wasn't lost on Sam that as these scenes unfolded, Daniel was still smiling. But his smile was now a little weary, a little apologetic, perhaps even a little embarrassed. It was almost painful for Sam to watch.

Later that night, Daniel arrives home at the same six-story walk-up. He climbs the stairs and enters the apartment, which is cluttered with a bike, a crib, toys. Dropping his backpack on the floor, he enters the small kitchen, where his wife has one child in her arms and another at her knee. There is suddenly a loud thumping of dance music coming from overhead. Daniel looks at his wife as a tear of exhaustion falls down her cheek.

Cut to the following morning in Century Tower, where Daniel walks past the warren of cubicles, enters the corner office—now occupied by his old friend—and simply says: "I quit."

The music swells with the sound of cellos, or violas, Sam wasn't sure which. But it was definitely the swelling of strings.

Daniel and his wife are in the same old station wagon, but this time with their two children in the back and their belongings on the roof. Heading in the opposite direction, they cross the same bridge, which leads them to a highway and then a series of increasingly rural roads. Again, Daniel and his wife lean forward to look out the windshield, but now it's to admire the foliage. In a small town—somewhere in Vermont, perhaps—they pass a white church and a firehouse and then a local elementary school, where a posted sign reads NOW HIRING. When they climb out of their car in front of a modest little home, Daniel puts his hand around his wife's waist as their two-year-old toddles across the grass.

Fade to black.

—

When the lights came up, HT was already looking at Sam.

"Terrific, right?"

Sam didn't know what to say. His head was reeling a bit. Maybe it was the gin. But there was also something profoundly unnerving about watching thirty years of a life—of your own child's life—condensed into a matter of minutes.

"What was that?" he ended up asking. "A law firm? An advertising firm?"

"Does it matter?"

"Doesn't it?"

HT spun in his chair to look at Sam more directly as he clarified his remark. "It's not like we have a crystal ball, Sam. This is just a projection—a carefully engineered and statistically supported projection—but a projection nonetheless. It's designed to give you a sense of the *contours* of Daniel's life, not the exact specifics. So, is it a law firm or an ad firm? We don't know. But given his genetic makeup and likely upbringing, we're fairly confident that, after attending a competitive, midsize liberal-arts college, *this* Daniel would become a young professional in a leading urban center. So, yes. Working in a law firm or ad firm or consulting firm. In Chicago or Atlanta or San Francisco. These are basically variables and, regardless of which ones Daniel chooses, he will probably end up with a similar life experience. But let's not get too bogged down in the weeds. What did you think more *generally*?"

"It was very satisfying in the beginning," Sam admitted after a moment. "I liked the picture it painted of him. But it was hard to watch him reach his thirties with so little to show for his efforts. Professionally, I mean."

"Sure," said HT, nodding and shifting his expression to a sober acknowledgment. "It's a classic second-act setback."

HT kept nodding.

Sam furrowed his brow. "What do you mean?"

"You know. A second-act setback—in which, having started confidently along a particular trajectory, we come face-to-face with our own limitations."

"Is that necessary?"

HT shrugged in the manner of one who didn't make up the rules. "To some degree it's unavoidable. We're all born with certain strengths which, ideally, are fostered by our parents and positively reinforced through education and peer interaction. But our strengths don't serve us well in every circumstance at every phase of our lives. As we grow and enter new contexts, our longer-term strengths can suddenly hamper our worldly progress, which in turn can create dissonance at home. When we find ourselves in that situation, eventually we have to confront the fact that the way we've approached life in the past is not effective in our current situation. Just as Daniel has to recognize that his good-natured predisposition which served him so well in his youth, may not serve him as well when he is an urban professional in a competitive field."

HT's tone shifted back to enthusiastic.

"Now, there are some personalities who, faced with this realization, might try to transform themselves into someone they are not. What I love about Annie's choice is that, in this version of Daniel, he embraces who he has been from the start. Rather than changing his behavior, he changes his context. He picks up his family and moves to a world where his virtues are more closely aligned with a path to happiness. We are who we are, right? There's no point in pushing our personalities uphill."

Pushing our personalities uphill …

Upon hearing this pithy phrase, rather than thinking about it in relation to Daniel, Sam found himself thinking about it in relation to his wife. Annie had attended a competitive, midsize liberal-arts college—not unlike the one depicted in the projection—where she had majored in English and written a thesis on divine ambiguity, or something, in the poetry of Emily Dickinson. And though she had gone on to graduate from law school and land a position at a white-shoe firm, recently she seemed to be taking more pleasure in her pro bono work than her corporate practice. In choosing this projection, was Annie expressing some sort of regret about the life they had chosen to make for themselves in the city rather than in some small bucolic town?

HT was watching Sam, studying his expression. "What do you say? Are you ready for number two? Or do you want to take a break?"

"No, I'm good," said Sam. "I'm ready."

"Great."

PROJECTION
TWO

WHEN THE LIGHTS DIMMED, Sam drank the rest of his gin and tonic. Once again, the Vitek logo receded and the name Daniel appeared then the projection began. This time the narrator was a man.

From the day he was born, Daniel marched to the beat of his own drum ...

After a shot of a swaddled baby with a furrowed brow, there followed a series of clips. At the age of four, Daniel explains rather earnestly, as if he's put some thought into the matter, that he doesn't actually need a nap right now. At the age of fifteen, Daniel asks his English teacher: "Isn't the only reason *we're* reading *Tom Sawyer* and *The Great Gatsby* in high school because you read *Tom Sawyer* and *The Great Gatsby* in high school?" At the age of twenty-two, Daniel is in the office of a college dean who wants to know why he missed his political-science exam.

"Because I was writing poetry," he answers matter-of-factly.

"Couldn't that have waited?"

"Waited for what?"

On the screen the dean frowns, but in the theater Sam laughs.

Daniel is sitting now in the same station wagon from the first projection, but in place of a pretty blonde, there is a beat-up Smith Corona in the passenger seat. As Daniel pulls away from the curb, in the near distance can be seen the rest of his classmates in graduation gowns throwing their caps in the air. Daniel drives over the same bridge into the same city. He enters the same six-story walk-up with his typewriter under one arm and a duffel bag under the other, holding the door open for no one. Once again, Daniel arrives at Century Tower and double-checks the address in his hand. But this time, after looking up at the building's gleaming surface, he says: "Fuck that." Tossing the address in a trash can, he continues down the street with his hands tucked in his pockets.

Suddenly, we hear the unmistakable opening chords of Bob Dylan's "Like a Rolling Stone." As the music plays, there is a montage showing Daniel's life in the city: washing dishes in a Chinese restaurant; drinking in a run-down bar with a ragtag group of friends; typing in his one-room apartment late into the night; and sending off a manuscript, which, after landing on an anonymous desk, is stamped with the single word *reject*.

As Dylan's anthem plays on, the series of images repeats itself: dishes, drinking, typing, rejection. The third time the series begins, the music fades into the background so we can hear Daniel being reprimanded by his boss in the restaurant's kitchen. "Fuck this," Daniel says, throwing his apron on the floor. In the run-down joint where he hangs out with his friends, there is now a group of yuppies crowding the bar. When one of them tells Daniel that smoking isn't allowed, Daniel pops him in the nose. And when, a moment later, Daniel is thrown into the street by the bouncer, Daniel shouts back, "Fuck you."

Sam couldn't help but note with a touch of parental concern that since dropping out of college, this Daniel has only said three sentences and *fuck* has been the verb in each one of them.

Cut to a beleaguered Daniel sitting motionless before his typewriter with a cigarette hanging from his lips, a bottle of bourbon close at hand, and another finished manuscript on the table. After an uncomfortable wait, Daniel types a few words and pulls the page from the typewriter. A close-up shows the title of his new book: *Fuck You, America*. But this time, on the anonymous desk the manuscript is stamped with the word *buy*.

Here the sequence of images accelerates. Presses run. Copies of the book are stacked in a bookstore with signs referring to the "Runaway Bestseller." At a Beverly Hills hotel, Daniel shakes hands with a movie star to whom he has just optioned the book. At the premiere, he exits the theater on the arm of the lead actress. In the Hollywood Hills, a broker hands him the keys to a striking Mid-Century Modern home. When Daniel walks inside, the camera pans the landscape to a billboard for *Fuck You, America*. In the background the clouds begin speeding by. Night comes and goes several times and the image on the billboard transforms to announce the sequel: *Fuck You Too, Europe*.

The camera now shifts to Sunset Boulevard, where Daniel is driving in a roadster late at night, weaving in and out of his lane. On a winding canyon road, he crashes into his own mailbox and stumbles up his driveway past an array of luxury cars as blood trickles down his forehead. Inside the house there is a chaotic party that looks like it's been going on for days. Daniel grabs a bottle of bourbon from the bar, retreats into his room, sits on his bed, and takes a healthy swig.

Morning. A close-up of Daniel's face, hungover and ill shaven with a little dried blood on his brow. The camera pulls back to reveal that he is lying on the floor. When his bloodshot eyes open, he sees a bulky shape in the shadows under his bed. As he squints, the shape comes into focus. It's the Smith Corona. A knowing smile begins to form on Daniel's face.

Cut to black.

This time when the lights came up, it was Sam who was already looking at HT.

"Are you kidding?"

HT was taken aback by Sam's tone. "Kidding about what?"

Sam pointed at the screen. "Annie saw this?"

"Of course, she saw it. She *chose* it. It really struck a chord with her."

"Struck a chord!"

HT turned a little in his chair. "What is it, Sam? What's on your mind?"

"The clear implication at the end of this projection is that Daniel is miserable."

"Okay," said HT, nodding. "But I'd put it a little differently. You're absolutely right that, given the nature of Daniel's success, his life seems to have become adorned with empty luxuries and false relationships. But it's the very hollowness of these adornments that allows him to see his situation for what it is."

"And I'm supposed to take heart from that."

"Absolutely!"

HT turned around more in his chair to look back at the projection booth. "Hey, Harry! Bring up the closing shot."

The face of the second Daniel reappeared on the screen, looking generally the worse for wear.

"See that smile, Sam? Isn't it enviable? I mean, he's just had a vision of what is important in life. I love the visual subtext of this shot because what is Daniel looking at right now? His typewriter! During all those years when he was toiling away in a kitchen, living in a walk-up, writing books that no one wanted to read, there was scarcity and rejection, but there was freedom and authenticity too."

HT shook his head in satisfaction.

"I think we can assume that his life is about to veer in a terrific direction."

Sam stared at the frozen image of Daniel, following his own train of thought. What could it mean that Annie had chosen *this* projection? At some level, Sam couldn't help but take it personally. He too had gone to a competitive liberal-arts college, where, as a freshman, he had studied Shakespeare and dabbled in poetry—just like everybody else. And yes, he had eventually chosen economics as his major and written his thesis on John Maynard Keynes. But did that make him some sort of sellout? Would he be more *free* and *authentic* if he were a dishwasher and they lived in a one-room apartment?

"Are you ready for the third projection?" asked HT.

"I'm ready for a second gin and tonic."

HT, who always seemed so ready to please, hesitated. "Are you sure you want another?"

"Pretty sure."

"Having said that a drink can be additive to the experience, Sam, we've found that a second drink can be a little reductive."

"I think I can handle it."

HT, the counselor, adopted an expression of friendly concern.

Sam, the customer, held up his glass and rattled the ice cubes.

So, James was summoned in his catering clothes, and a second drink was promptly delivered.

"Are you ready now?" HT asked, a little coolly.

Sam put a finger in the air while he drank a third of the G&T. Then putting down the glass, he said, "Let her rip."

PROJECTION THREE

FROM THE DAY THAT DANIEL WAS BORN, *everything came easy* ...

As the narrator—who was a woman again—elaborated on Daniel's "natural finesse," there was a montage showing the ease with which he made friends, played sports, and pursued academics.

The skeptic in Sam wanted to roll his eyes at the screen's portrayal of the effortless Daniel. But hadn't he encountered just this sort of person in college—like his freshman roommate, John. Raised in Wilmington and educated at St. Paul's, John seemed to meet every new task with a knack. Sam vividly remembered the afternoon when John first tried his hand at lacrosse. Having watched some others playing on the quad, John picked up a stick and in a matter of minutes was cradling, throwing, and catching with the fluency of a varsity player—the way some young musicians can drop one instrument and pick up another without bothering to pause for instruction.

Sam was nothing like John. But our genes don't merely express who we are. They contain all manner of talents from previous generations that we may not benefit from personally but that can be passed on to our progeny. So, who was to say that he couldn't father a son with the natural finesse of his old classmate?

As Sam was having this reassuring thought, the setting shifted from a university campus to Century Tower, where Daniel, already in his early thirties, dressed in a tailored suit, is walking down the hallway with a smile on his face and some folders under an arm. Passing a colleague of a similar age in similar attire, Daniel exchanges a high five. Then he pauses at a cubicle where another young man is transferring data from a document into a spreadsheet. When the young man looks up, Sam realizes with a touch of horror that it is the same actor who played Daniel in the first projection. The new Daniel dumps the folders on the old Daniel's desk while making some smug remark about there being no rest for the weary.

Later that night (as Daniel One is presumably toiling away) Daniel Three is sitting in a fancy restaurant charming his waitress. A moment after she slips him her phone number, another attractive young woman arrives, gives Daniel a kiss, and sits. When Daniel reaches across the table to take her hand, on her finger we see the engagement ring that he has given her.

The scene shifts back to the office, where a paralegal emerges from the copy room straightening her skirt, followed by a smiling Daniel, who is straightening his tie. When Daniel returns to his sizable office he finds a superior waiting.

"Can I see you for a moment, Danno?"

Danno? thought Sam.

Danno is led into a conference room where there are two other senior professionals, a man from HR and a woman from Legal. He is invited to take a seat.

"It has been brought to our attention," says the man from HR, "that this summer you may have been sleeping with one of the interns …"

"Two," says the woman from Legal.

"Two of the interns."

"As I remember," Daniel replies with a wink, "we didn't get much sleep."

Cut to Daniel being led from his office by security with a cardboard box in his arms. As he passes between the cubicles, several of the analysts stand and applaud, including Daniel One.

The following montage is painfully easy for Sam to anticipate. Daniel having the engagement ring thrown in his face before his fiancée slams the door; Daniel applying for jobs he can't get; Daniel ending his nights alone in a loft that seems glamorous but cold.

A year goes by, maybe two. Chastened, humbled, near defeat,

Daniel is standing in a small office building reading the tenancy board until he finds the firm of McClintock & Co. Upstairs, he enters a waiting room with run-down furniture and an empty reception desk.

"Can I help you?" asks the sixty-year-old African American woman who emerges from an office.

"Yes," says Daniel. "I'm interested in speaking with Mr. McClintock."

"*I'm* Mr. McClintock," the woman says sourly.

Daniel clears his throat.

"Excuse me, Ms. McClintock. I have almost a decade of experience in the field and I was hoping you might have an opening ..."

"The only opening we've got," she says, pointing at the reception desk, "is the one right there."

"I'll take it," says Daniel.

"All right, all right!" Sam called out. "I get it! Enough already!"

As Harry froze the projection and brought up the lights, HT turned to Sam in surprise.

"Don't you want to see what happens next? It's the best part!"

"Oh, I can just imagine," said Sam. "At the foot of his wise new mentor, Daniel learns to be a better man."

"Exactly," said HT. "Terrific, right?"

"But why does he have to be such an asshole to become a good person?"

"It's a classic second act, Sam. In the beginning——"

"Let me stop you right there, HT. What is it with all this *classic second act* business? We're not talking about a Hollywood movie."

"Of course we're not talking about a Hollywood movie, Sam. We're talking about your son's life. But where do you think the three-act structure comes from? And why does it consistently speak to audiences? Because it's an archetype. A universal pattern that recurs one generation after another. It's not a coincidence that when the Sphinx poses his riddle to Oedipus, the answer is the three phases of man."

"Oedipus! You do know that he slept with his mother and killed his father."

"Okay," said HT, putting up his hands. "Maybe not that best example. It goes without saying that our lives are intricate and multi-faceted. But they also tend to have a larger arc that takes us from a position of youthful self-assurance through a period of setbacks, leading to a third phase in which, if we're lucky, we've confronted our limitations and become deeper people ready to lead richer lives."

"And because Daniel is someone for whom things came easy, he ends up being an asshole?"

"Not 'ends up,' Sam. He's an asshole *to begin with*. But by the time he confronts the callousness of his own personality, he still has years—maybe half a century—in which to put his talents to more meaningful use. What a terrific third act! Are you kidding me? I would have happily been an asshole for thirty years in order to be wise for another fifty."

Sam wasn't sure where he should go with that admission. In the end, he just shook his head in exasperation. "I think your whole premise is crazy. Not all lives play out like that. It's not like I've had to spend the last fifteen years drunk or philandering in order to prepare for my third act."

HT, who was listening intently, opened his mouth as if to comment, then uncharacteristically kept his counsel.

"What?" asked Sam.

"Nothing."

"Come on! What?"

HT shrugged. "You're sort of mixing apples and oranges. That's all."

"Why?"

"Because for the last fifteen years, you've been in your third act."

"Excuse me?"

"What can I tell you? We have your genetic makeup and your personality profile. We have your upbringing, your education, your career history, and we've mapped all that against our database of human outcomes. It seems very clear to us that your second act was back in college."

"College!"

"Sometimes that's when it happens, Sam. It's like you told our interviewers. You had an idyllic childhood in a nice house in the suburbs and summers by the sea. But then your father quit his corporate engineering job, bought the copper mine, moved the family to Utah, and that's when the troubles began. Wait. How did you describe him?" HT opened the green file and flipped quickly to somewhere in the middle. *"No promise was ever quite kept; no bill ever quite paid; no dream ever quite realized."*

"I know what it says."

Sensing from Sam's tone that he had gone a step too far, HT resumed in a more sympathetic manner. "You went through an extraordinary series of experiences in your college years, Sam. While others were focused on getting drunk and getting laid, you were helping your father renegotiate with vendors, lay off employees, plead with banks, and navigate bankruptcy. And in so doing, you had to come to terms with the fact that the man you had idolized your whole life was not exactly whom you had imagined him to be. In the aftermath of that experience, you made a promise that you would never put your family in the same position. You achieved in school, advanced in a competitive field, steered clear of higher-risk opportunities, and ensured that when you had children, they would be raised on a foundation of financial stability. That this is your third act is nothing to be ashamed of, Sam. You should be incredibly proud of where you are."

And Sam might even have felt some of that pride, if HT hadn't referenced his *steering clear of higher-risk opportunities.* Unlike so many of his colleagues, Sam had never attempted to shift to the buy side—to a private equity firm or hedge fund—where the analysts lived and died by their recommendations, but had the opportunity to accumulate *real* money. He hadn't even attempted a lateral move within the firm to a faster-growing sector like tech or telecom, wary of their rapidly changing competitive landscapes. Utilities may be regulated and slow-growing, as Sam liked to say to his clients, but they were also predictable and paid dividends.

But if HT's mention of these unpursued opportunities stung, it stung nothing like Sam's realization that he had never referenced them in any of his interviews with Vitek. If they were in that file, they must have come from Annie, presumably as examples of her husband's lack of ambition or grit.

Sam shook his head.

"Some of what you've said may be true," he admitted finally. "But I think Annie and I have another act ahead of us."

"Oh," replied HT. "I didn't say it was Annie's third act. We're fairly certain that she's still in her second."

WE WERE
JUST TALKING
ABOUT YOU

SAM SLAMMED THE DOOR of his new car. Or rather, he tried to slam it. But the door, like the motor, had been engineered to operate smoothly and quietly. So, when he tugged the door shut, it advanced, paused, and closed itself with an unobtrusive click.

"Fuck you," said Sam to the door.

He pushed the ignition and the car stirred to life with the slightest tremble. As if in harmony, the phone in Sam's pocket began to vibrate with an incoming call—presumably from Annie or the office. Ignoring it, Sam initiated the GPS.

Where would you like to go? it asked.

"Two hundred and ten East Eighty-Fifth Street."

Proceed to the highlighted route. Take a right onto Local Access Road then continue eight miles to the expressway entrance.

At Vitek's exit Sam came to a stop despite the fact there was no oncoming traffic. The GPS calculated that he would arrive back at the apartment at 7:34, in plenty of time for dinner. But Sam felt a sudden desire to turn left and follow the access road all the way to Orient Point—in order to visit that little house by the sea, the one that his parents had rented before his father quit his job, uprooted the family, and dragged them all out west.

Someone behind Sam honked.

Without signaling, Sam turned right and headed toward the city as it began to rain.

The access road, which ran parallel to the expressway, was lined with telephone poles that may or may not have been carrying telephone calls anymore. At one time, this road had presumably been the main artery extending from the city to the tip of the peninsula, but the expressway had turned it into a secondary route spotted with secondary businesses. Case in point, Sam was passing a motor lodge from the 1950s with a parking area that was three times bigger than it now needed to be.

Up ahead Sam saw another remnant of the access road's heyday: a bar advertising itself as The Glass Half Full, complete with an oversize neon sign of a tipped martini that loomed over an old school phone booth at the side of the road. As Sam drove by, he noticed that at the bottom of the martini glass was a neon olive that was no longer lit.

Sam pulled over onto the shoulder. After letting two cars pass, he did a three-point turn and headed back.

The GPS chimed to indicate its recalculation of the route home.

Take a left onto Maple Street, then proceed one-eighth of a mile and take a left onto Church Street.

Instead, Sam took a left into the parking lot of The Glass Half Full. It was also three times larger than it needed to be, accommodating a handful of pickup trucks and older American sedans. Sam got out of his car and walked quickly toward the door as the rain began to fall in earnest.

Inside, the ambience was defined by back-lit beer signs hanging on the walls and billiard balls clacking somewhere out of sight. On Sam's right was a row of booths being used by parties of two or three while on his left was a bar lined with men in work clothes sitting on stools. A few of the men turned and looked in a manner suggesting they were used to recognizing whomever came into the bar. When they saw it was Sam, they went back to their beers.

After letting his eyes adjust, Sam walked farther into the bar in search of a quiet place to sit. But as he proceeded, he was surprised to discover HT sitting in the fourth booth talking to a brunette. Sam didn't imagine The Glass Half Full was HT's sort of place. Maybe he'd just found that having a drink right after work was *additive to his experience*. Sam took a step toward him with every intention of making a wry remark to this effect, and that's when he realized that the brunette in the booth was Annie.

Sam stopped in confusion. He and Annie were planning to talk about their "options" over dinner later that night. Had she driven out to get a reading from HT on Sam's impressions in advance? But even as he was asking himself this question, Sam realized that resting on the table between two glasses of red wine were HT's and Annie's fingers interlinked.

Looking up, HT let go of Annie's hand.

"Sam!" he said in his upbeat way. "What perfect timing! We were just talking about you."

HT slid out of the booth and stood in order to shake Sam's hand.

Which was just as well, since it made it so much easier for Sam to punch him in the face. Sam had never hit another person. So, with all the sharpness of a brand-new experience, he could feel the bone in HT's nose breaking and he could see HT's head snapping back as he slumped into the booth.

There was a rap on the glass.

"Hey! You okay in there, buddy?"

Sam looked out the passenger side window to find someone peering into the car. It was an ill-shaven man in his late fifties holding a newspaper over his head to fend off the rain. Sam lowered the window.

"You okay?" the man asked again.

"Yeah," said Sam. "I'm fine. Thanks."

"All righty," the man said before limping toward the bar.

Sam sat for a minute watching the windshield wipers sweep back and forth, his spirits lifted by the punch he hadn't thrown. Then he followed the stranger inside.

The Glass Half Full was almost as he had imagined it. Though there was a pool table in the back, there were no balls in play; and though there was a bar on the left and booths on the right, there were also a few tables for four in between; and though there were, in fact, a number of men in work clothes seated on the stools, none of them bothered to look up when Sam came through the door.

Sam sat at the near corner of the bar, a few stools away from the man who had rapped on his window. A Motown song was playing on the jukebox in the corner, something by the Temptations or the Four Tops. Sam could never remember which was which.

"A gin and tonic," he said to the bartender while setting his phone facedown on the bar. "Or, on second thought, make that a martini."

"You have a preference for gin?"

"Whatever you've got on the top shelf."

Another Motown song began playing, and Sam drummed on the bar, pleased with his ability to remember, or anticipate, the song's infectious rhythms. But when the bartender returned with a martini served on the rocks in a whiskey glass, Sam couldn't help but feel disappointed.

"That'll be ten bucks," said the bartender.

"Can I have it straight up?"

"We don't have any martini glasses."

"But what about the sign?"

"What sign?"

Sam considered explaining, but a large fellow in a baseball cap who was seated to his right turned to look him over.

"This is perfect," Sam conceded as his phone began to vibrate again. "In fact, why don't you set another one in motion."

THE GLASS
HALF FULL

SAM WAS DRUNK. He could tell he was drunk because he was losing track of things. He'd lost track of the time. He'd lost track of how many "martinis" he'd had and how many times his phone had buzzed on the bar. He also couldn't remember when the ill-shaven man—whose name was Beezer—had moved to the stool on his left, or how they had come to be talking about Sam's father.

"A copper mine!" exclaimed Beezer, slurring his words. "I'd love to own a copper mine."

"Believe me," said Sam, slurring them back, "a mine is the last thing you'd love to own."

Beezer looked incredulous, so Sam began ticking off reasons.

"Mature industry ... Undifferentiated product ... Labor-intensive ... Economically sensitive ..."

Sam paused with a thumb and three fingers in the air, certain there was a fifth reason.

Meanwhile, Beezer nodded with the expression of one who was keenly interested but only half following.

"If all you say is true," he asked, "then why would your old man buy one?"

"It was his dream," said Sam, putting the word "dream" in its place by adding a pair of air quotes. Sam took a drink then looked at his neighbor. "You want to know *how* bad the mining business is?"

"Sure."

"One afternoon, when I was a senior in high school, my old man withdrew all our savings from the bank, drove six hours to Vegas, put the bundle on black, and let it ride: Six … times … in a row."

"No shit," said Beezer. "You hearing this, Nick?"

The bartender, who was drying a glass, said: "I'm hearing it."

Sam leaned toward Beezer. "Do you know what the odds are of black coming up on a roulette wheel six times in a row?"

Beezer shook his head.

"One in seventy-six. And with that once-in-a-lifetime stroke of good fortune, my father staved off the inevitable for another fourteen months."

Sam raised his martini.

"To Chapter Eleven," he said, then emptied the glass.

"Well, it looks like everything worked out," said Beezer,

gesturing to Sam's suit and then toward the parking lot, presumably in the direction of the car.

"If everything worked out," said Sam, "it was no thanks to my dad. That car out there, this suit …"

Sam shook his head without finishing his sentence. Then he shifted to a different point.

"I am forty-five years old, and I'm about to have my very first kid. And do you know why that is? Because I waited. I waited until I had money in my pocket, a cushion in the bank, and a three-bedroom apartment on the Upper East Side with no mortgage. That's why!"

"You're having a kid!" exclaimed Beezer, as if it were the only thing he had heard.

"We're in the process … ," said Sam with a wave of the hand. "That's why I'm out here."

The smile left Beezer's face. "That's why you're out where?"

"In one mile, take Exit 46 then bear left," mimicked Sam.

"You mean Vitek?"

"None other."

Beezer turned away from Sam to look at Nick in a meaningful way. At least, in a drunken sort of meaningful way. Then he turned back to Sam. "That's one of them fertility clinics, right?"

"Not 'one of,'" corrected Sam. "It's *the* fertility clinic."

"So, how does it work in there? You pay the fare and then you get to pick if it's a boy or a girl, blue-eyed or brown?"

Sam laughed. "Boy or blue, girl or brown, that stuff's for amateurs. At Vitek, you get to pick your kid's *contours.*"

"Contours?"

"What sort of temperament he's gonna have. What sort of career. What sort of life."

"Top-shelf," said Nick.

Sam looked at the bartender. He wanted to ask what sort of crack that was supposed to be, but Beezer spoke first.

"It's just like I told you, Nick."

Sam looked back at Beezer. "Told him what?"

Beezer leaned closer to Sam. "You know when Vitek opened?"

"About a year ago … ?"

"That's right. But do you know what was in their building for the ten years before that?"

"No."

"Raytheon."

After letting this sink in, Beezer elaborated: "The Raytheon Company of Waltham, Massachusetts. One of the largest defense contractors in the world. For ten years they're in that building with people coming and going at all hours of day and night. Then one morning last September, suddenly all the cars are gone, the building goes dark, and the sign comes down. Two weeks later, the parking lot's full, the lights are back on, and the sign says *Vitek, Incorporated.*"

Beezer gave Sam the nod of mutual understanding.

Sam gave Beezer the shake of solitary confusion.

"Two weeks later!" said Beezer. "Doesn't that seem a little surprising to you? That one corporation could empty out a building overnight and a totally new corporation could take its place in fourteen days? There's only one way that happens. And that's if there was never any change in occupancy at all. And Vitek, Incorporated, isn't really Vitek, Incorporated. It's a *division* of Raytheon."

Beezer leaned a little closer.

"Which, when you think about it, sort of figures."

"Sort of figures how?"

"Because genetics is the future of defense."

Sam had already gotten the sense that Beezer was a little crazy, but a chill ran down his spine nonetheless.

"They don't call it birth control for nothing," said Beezer. Then after taking a drink of his beer, he added, "I've got it all written down."

"What you've got," said Nick, "is too much time on your hands."

Beezer ignored Nick's comment and squinted at Sam. "Let me

ask you something: To do this fertility stuff, did they hand you a dirty magazine and send you into a little room and ask you for a sample?"

"Something like that," said Sam.

"But they called it a *sample*, right?"

"I think so."

Beezer nodded with the smile of the known-it-all-along. "That choice of words is no coincidence. They call it a *sample* because they want you to think it's some little representative part of something else. But what you're giving them isn't some little representative part of something else. It's *the thing*. In fact, it's the whole kit and caboodle."

Sam looked at Beezer, impressed by the majesty of his mania. Then he turned to Nick. "How about another round for me and my neighbor here?"

Nick looked at Sam. "Don't you think you've had enough?"

"Just one more?" asked Sam, trying to smile in the manner of Daniel One.

Or maybe it was in the manner of Daniel Three.

Either way, he smiled.

"I'll tell you what," said Nick. "I'll bring you a glass of water. Drink that first, then we can talk about another round."

"Whatever you say, barkeep."

As Nick went to get the glass of water, Sam's phone began to vibrate on the bar.

"Hey, buddy," said Beezer, "it's your phone again. That's gotta be the tenth time it's buzzed. Maybe you'd better answer it."

Sam looked around.

"Do you hear something buzzing?" Then picking the phone up off the bar, he dangled it over his glass of water and let it drop. "Because I don't hear any—"

But before Sam could finish, the big fellow on his right put a hand on his shoulder, turned him around, and punched out his lights.

LOOSE CHANGE

FLAT ON HIS BACK, Sam opened his eyes to find a bright light staring down from overhead.

Oh my God, he thought. *I'm on an operating table!*

But then the ill-shaven visage of Beezer leaned into view.

"Hey, Nick. He's back!"

Now the bartender leaned into view.

"Hallelujah," he said.

Sam began to move, but Nick put a hand on his shoulder. "Why don't you just stay put for a minute, friend. You took a tumble and hit your head."

Despite Nick's suggestion, Sam swung his legs to his right and sat up on the bar. As he tried to put the pieces together, he noticed that the jukebox wasn't playing, that there was blood on his shirt, and that most of the barstools were empty—including the one where the big guy in the baseball cap had been sitting.

"That man hit me!" said Sam, pointing an accusatory finger at the empty stool.

"Who?" said Nick. "Tony?"

"The big guy who was sitting right there. I put my phone in my water and just like that, he spun me around and hit me."

"What you put your phone in was Tony's vodka and soda. So …" Nick gave the shrug of universal absolution.

With Beezer's help, Sam climbed down from the bar. In the mirror behind Nick he saw that the area around his left eye had begun to swell.

"That's gonna be quite a shiner," acknowledged Nick.

"I've never had a shiner."

"Well, there you go," said Beezer with a grin. "They don't call it The Glass Half Full for nothing!"

When Sam sat back on his old stool, Nick put a plastic bag filled with ice on the bar and a martini beside it.

"Here," said Nick. "This one's on the house."

"I never drank my water."

"You've sobered up just the same."

As Sam put the bag against the side of his face, he watched Nick going about his business.

"You don't like me, do you?"

"I don't know you."

"Science says we can form lasting impressions of people in as short as two minutes," said Sam.

"Is that so?"

"That's true," said Beezer. "I read it in a magazine."

"Listen, Nick … Can I call you Nick?"

"You can call me whatever you want."

"I know we don't know each other. And I'm sorry if I've rubbed you the wrong way. But I'd still like to know why."

Nick gave Sam another look, as if he were sizing him up with a little more care. Then after nodding twice, mostly to himself, he put both hands on the bar.

"My wife and I have been married for thirty-four years," he began. "We grew up in the next town over and got pregnant when we were twenty-one. At the time, I had a job as a long-haul trucker, a union job making ten bucks an hour, and Betty was working at the hospital. We saved a little money and bought a little place with a little backyard figuring that maybe, God willing, we'd have a second kid. But the second kid? It turned out to be triplets. Identical twin boys and a girl. I didn't even know that shit could happen. With four kids under the age of three, I had to give up the long-haul trucking and Betty gave up the nursing. But we made it work. I got a local job in construction and painted houses on the weekends. The kids grew up eating mac and cheese and going to public school, the three boys sleeping in one room and Sally in another. But along the way, my wife and I realized that Sally—the runt of the litter—was the smart one. Smarter than any of her brothers. Smarter than either of us. So, we decided to send her to private school. We squeezed the lemon a little harder. And sure enough, by senior year she's placing at the top of her class and speaking three different languages. She gets into motherfucking Yale. Sure, we get some financial aid, but it's middle-class financial aid, which is to say, not enough. So, we have to sit the boys down and explain that we're all going to make some sacrifices. The twins are going to have to look at state schools or maybe work for a couple of years before college. Which is what they do, more or less, with no complaints. Then in the middle of her junior year, our little Sally comes home for Christmas and she can't get out of bed. She stays in her room half the day with the shades drawn, saying she doesn't want to go outside. She certainly doesn't want to go back to Yale. So, we get her a therapist—another squeeze of the lemon. Two months go by and Sally's therapist says that what Sally needs is for everyone to sit down together. Not just me and Betty, you understand, but all six of us. Ed's gotta get a special leave from his unit at Camp Pendleton, Jimmy takes the bus home from SUNY Oswego, and Billy comes up from Fort Lauderdale, where he's waiting tables during the day and going to culinary school at night. But they all come back. And we crowd together into this therapist's little office. And it's awkward. Nobody's saying anything. Ten minutes go by, maybe fifteen. But then suddenly, one of them says something and the four of them start talking. They talk about their childhoods. They say what they think about us and what they think about each other. The say what they think about themselves. And you know something? That was the most interesting day of my life."

Nick picked up Sam's empty glass.

"So, yeah. When all is said and done, I suppose your father's more my kind of guy."

Sam understood that this last remark was meant to be a slap in the face, and that's what it felt like. He stood up from the stool, nearly knocking it over. He took two brand-new hundred-dollar bills from his wallet and made a show of tossing them on the bar. Then he walked out of The Glass Half Full and into the pouring rain.

As he jogged across the lot toward his car, Sam was already regretting throwing the money on the bar. Nick was bound to take it as proof of all his worst suspicions about guys in custom suits and fancy cars. But Sam hadn't thrown the money on the bar to show off his wealth. He had thrown it to show that he was the sort of man who didn't need to drive six hours to Las Vegas and beat improbable odds just so he could keep a folly of his own invention on life support.

Sam climbed into his car and yanked the door, which eased to a close as the rain poured in on the upholstery. When he pushed the ignition, Sam happened to glance at the clock and saw that he was already two hours late.

"Shit."

Taking his phone from his pocket, Sam pressed the side button, but to no effect. It took him a moment to realize that the phone wasn't responding because he had submerged it in Tony's vodka and soda.

"Shit," he said again.

After shaking his head at this fiasco of his own making, Sam went to wipe the rain off his face, triggering a sharp pain in his cheek. Turning on the overhead light, he looked in the rearview mirror and saw that his shiner was coming along nicely. He could add that to the list of things he was going to have to explain when he got home. But even as he was having this thought, in the corner of the mirror he noticed the proud rectangular figure of the phone booth standing at the side of the road.

His spirits raised by the sight, Sam patted his pants and jacket pockets to see if he had any change—but of course he didn't. Who the hell had change anymore? He looked down into the tray beside the driver seat, but the car was too new to have accumulated the normal automotive detritus.

Stymied, Sam looked through the windshield.

He certainly wasn't going back into The Glass Half Full.

But there were still a few other vehicles in the parking lot …

After a moment, Sam got out of his car and slunk toward a nearby pickup that looked even older than the bar. For no good reason, it was locked. Sam moved on to a Chrysler sedan that needed a new paint job. The door handle gave, promisingly. Glancing back at the bar, Sam quickly opened the door, slipped into the driver's seat, and closed the door again so that the overhead light wouldn't be on for more than a second. As it was dark, Sam reached into his jacket so that he could use the flashlight on his phone. This time, he remembered it was dead before he got it out of his pocket.

In the tray beside the driver's seat, there were two empty coffee cups. Setting them on the passenger's seat, Sam reached into the cup holders and felt two dimes stuck to the bottom. They were so stuck, he had to use his fingernails to pry them free. Sam had no idea what a phone call to the city would cost, but it was certainly more than twenty cents. Cognizant that at any moment the owner of the car might emerge from the bar, Sam rifled through the glove compartment to no avail. Then, suddenly, he had a flash from childhood—a vision of raiding his father's car for loose change in the hopes of going to the movies. Turning ninety degrees, Sam shoved his fingers into the crease between the back and the bottom of the driver's seat. In a matter of seconds, he felt the unmistakable shape of two quarters. With his muscle memory taking over, Sam pinched the quarters between the tips of two fingers and eased them carefully from the crevice in which they were lodged.

The necessary change in hand, Sam opened the door of the sedan with every intention of getting quickly out. But just as he was sliding from behind the wheel, he noticed the two photographs taped to the dash. Both were of three boys and a girl. In the first picture, which was faded with age, the kids were around eight or nine and standing in front of a quaint little house. On their shoulders, they had oversize backpacks like it was the first day of school. In the second picture, they were standing in the same spot in the same arrangement, but now in their early twenties. It occurred to Sam that this picture was probably taken around the time that Sally had begun to struggle. As Nick had said, she was the runt of the litter, standing half a foot shorter than her brothers. With a deep sense of shame, Sam realized that he had never bothered to ask Nick how his daughter had fared.

Climbing out of the bartender's car, Sam gave one last look over his shoulder, then ran to the booth at the edge of the lot. When he opened the door, he was startled to have the light go on, but then relieved.

"God bless the phone company," he said.

Holding the door open with a foot so that the light wouldn't go off, Sam put all of Nick's change in the slot and dialed Annie's cell.

But as soon as he heard the call going through, he realized he'd made a big mistake. What he should have dialed was their landline—because Annie never carried her cell phone around the apartment. When she got home, she invariably put it on the credenza by the front door, along with her keys and her wallet. Even if she heard the phone ringing, she would never make it across the apartment in time.

Sure enough, after five rings the phone went to voicemail.

Sam couldn't remember how long a payphone call lasted, but when the beep came, he didn't waste any time. He told Annie he was sorry. He told her he was sorry that he was late, sorry that he hadn't made it for dinner, sorry that he hadn't been able to call. There were other things he was sorry about too, but worried that he was running out of time, he paused, expecting a recorded voice to interrupt, demanding twenty-five cents for another two minutes.

But Sam hadn't run out of time, and he found himself standing there holding the receiver to his ear without speaking—like some-one who was waiting for the person at the other end of the line to respond.

"Annie, I'm so sorry," he finally began, but the line went dead.

Sam stepped out of the phone booth into the rain and found himself looking up at the neon sign. Maybe his eyes were playing tricks on him, or maybe some of the neon tubing momentarily reflected the headlights of an oncoming car, but Sam was almost certain that for one clear second the olive at the bottom of the martini glass blinked on.

After staring for a moment, Sam strode to his car. Letting the door close at its own pace, he pushed the ignition and drove to the exit.

Where would you like to go? asked the GPS.

But Sam turned off the system. He didn't need it to tell him how to get to where he was going.

A TABLE
FOR FOUR

AT 10:45, Nick and Beezer were sitting alone in the empty bar at one of the four-tops with a cup of coffee and a glass of beer. It was closing time, more or less, and Nick had some cleaning up to do, so he should probably have sent Beezer on his way, but it was still raining and Beezer didn't have a car, so Nick decided to give him one on the house while he was having his coffee. On occasion, Nick did that—let Beezer stay for a while after closing, as long as he didn't talk too much.

As they sat there drinking quietly, reflectively, the door to The Glass Half Full swung open and in walked Mr. Contours, drenched to the bone. Standing in the doorway, he gave the bar a once-over. Then he put a hand in his suit pocket and began advancing toward their table. For a moment, Nick wondered if this crazy bastard had returned with a gun. Beezer must have thought the same thing, because his face went white. But when Contours reached their table, he collapsed into the chair across from Nick and, without saying a word, took his hand from his pocket and slammed something down. When he removed his hand, there in the middle of the table, illuminated by an overhead lamp, was a small plastic container, at the bottom of which was a pale white substance.

"Holy shit!" said Beezer, pushing his chair back with a jolt, like it was some kind of explosive.

"Well, I'll be damned," said Nick.

Contours didn't look smug. He didn't look smart or victorious. He looked like someone on the verge of a resolution.

Without Nick or Beezer asking, he explained that when he went back to Vitek, he had to bang on the door for fifteen minutes before a security guard would let him in. It took another fifteen minutes to get some guy named HT on the phone so that he could get back his kit and caboodle.

When he finished talking, neither Nick nor Beezer spoke. The three of them sat there in silence, not looking at each other so much as at the middle of the table—at that small plastic container in which there was and wasn't their future. In which there was and wasn't ours.

ABOUT THE AUTHOR

Amor Towles's novel, *A Gentleman in Moscow* was on the New York Times bestseller list for over a year in hardcover and was named one of the best books of 2016 by the Chicago Tribune, the Washington Post, the Philadelphia Inquirer, the San Francisco Chronicle, and NPR. The book has been translated into over thirty-five languages including Russian. In the summer of 2017, the novel was optioned by director Tom Harper to for a 16-hour miniseries starring Kenneth Branagh. Mr. Towles lives in Manhattan.